FANTASTICALLY QUEER BEASTS AND MAGICS

By

Mrs. Arthur H. D. Acland

Updated By

A.D. Padgett

Published by
ADP Publishing

First Published 2015
Copyright Anthony Padgett 2015

QUEER BEASTS AND MAGICS
First Published 1918

ISBN 978-0-9572919-7-3

Dedication by Mrs. Arthur H. D. Acland:

To

DICK, ARTHUR, PHILIP, PETER,
MATTHEW AND MICHAEL

WHO GATHERED, IN WAR-TIME, AROUND A
CERTAIN
HEARTH IN CHELSEA TO ROAST AND EAT
APPLES,
AND TO LISTEN IN SEMI-DARKNESS TO
TALES
SO CALLED " BLOODCURDLING,"

THIS SMALL BOOK IS DEDICATED BY THEIR
GRATEFUL HOSTESS

Dedication by A.D. Padgett:

To

FORGOTTEN AND LARGELY FORGOTTEN WRITERS

TABLE OF CONTENTS

INTRODUCTION

"Queer Beasts and Magics" was published in 1918 and has been out of print until recently.

To bring the work to a new readership I've made the animals and beasts more fantastical and mythological, hence its new title of "Fantastically Queer Beasts and Magics".

The rat was a mouse, the Imp was a monkey, the Twolf was a hyena, the Lady Minotaur was a cow, the Centaur was a camel, the Merogre was a hippopotamus and the Hellephant was an elephant.

I've also created some minor edits and hope that if you enjoy this work you will find out original copies of the work to enjoy these also.

Let the magic begin...

Anthony Padgett

CHAPTER 1

THE EXCHANGE

THERE was once a young man called John Lang.

He loved the country, but had never been able to live there since he was a little boy, when his parents, who were now dead, had to go and live in a town.

Ever since he could work he had saved every penny he could, so as to be able to go back into the country and start afresh there. Up to the time when our story begins he had not been able to manage this. He had had to buy himself some furniture for one thing, but he did not mind that much, as "furniture," he said to himself, "wilt-be useful anywhere."

So here we find John Lang working away all day in the office of a factory in the middle of a huge town. Working there all day, and sleeping in a basement room of the factory at night, so as to earn a little more money by helping to take care of the buildings.

It was the most dismal place you ever saw, was that basement bedroom of his! The sun never shone into it. And as to the moon - why, the only way John Lang could get a glimpse of that was by going up into the street and watching for it to peep out behind the chimney-pots.

It was a wearying sort of life to live, and though John Lang - as you will see as the story goes on - was a plucky sort of fellow, he did long to get away from it. It was so lonely too. For as his work went on all day in the factory, and as he had no relations, he was very solitary when everyone else went home in the evenings.

This sort of thing had gone on for some time when a t last a change came.

John Lang was standing at the factory door looking up to the chimney-pots of the opposite houses and watching for a sight of the moon, which had been full the night before, when a man came briskly walking towards him. This man paused when he was close to John, and said "Good-evening" to him in a friendly sort of way.

"Good-evening to you," replied John; and then the two fell into a chat together. The man said he had come up from the country that day, and John was always glad of any chance to talk with anybody on that topic.

"How pleasant it must be in the country," said John. "Don't you love it?"

"No, I don't," said the man with a short laugh - "no, I don't."

"Oh," said John, "you are different from me. Now, I would give anything to live in the country."

"Why don't you go and live there, then?" asked the man.

"I can't," said John. "I have no house there - and I get my living here."

"But if you had a house and all sorts of chances in' the country, should you go there?"

"Of course I should," said John Lang.

"Would you?" said the man. "Then why shouldn't you exchange with me? I want to live in the town," he added, as if carelessly, but looking rather anxiously at John all the time.

"What do you mean?" asked John Lang.

"I mean," said the man, "that if you like I will change places with you, because I am tired of the country - tired of it. Yours seems to be just the sort of place I should like, and you seem to be tired of the town - so why not make an exchange? Look here," continued he, "this really is a good idea! You give me your things here - and I'll give what I've got in the country. It's really a jolly place. It's a house called Greenleas - there's a jolly garden and everything. You'd love that? You ask why I leave it? Well, I'll tell you I want to live in a town, and I want it so badly that I'll tell you what. I'll take the risk of your master engaging me when you've gone! Just you hand over anything you've got; and I'll hand over Greenleas to you. Then you'll have somewhere to go to, at all events - and I shall have a chance to settle in the town. See here! you and I will sign a bit of an agreement about this, and the thing's done!"

"Come down to my room and let's talk it over," said John, beginning to get excited. It really was worth while to talk things over, at all events, so he led the way, and the man followed, down the steep dark stairs into the small dark room where John slept. And as he went he felt more and more how like a prison it was to him, and more and more the memories of his childhood flooded into his mind, making his longing for the proposed change almost too great to resist.

Still he determined to be cautious, and watched quietly while the man from the country seized a piece of John Lang's office paper, took up a pen, dipped it in the ink and began writing hurriedly.

"There," said the man when he had finished writing. "There, sign that. Fetch a policeman or someone in to witness it, and you keep it. Let us have another like it for me to keep, and the thing is done."

John Lang took the paper and this is what he read:

"I agree to take over the country house called Greenleas, with all it contains and all that belongs to it, at once, in exchange for all my present possessions."

Nothing more.

It was tremendously tempting. The very thought of what the words "country house" meant made his heart thump, and he snatched up a pen and dipped it in the ink.

But - it was a great risk! Tempting, yes! But all the same a great risk. What if he should find, after having given up all his present possessions, that the whole thing was a hoax, and that there was no such place at all as Greenleas? These things wanted thought.

Toying with his pen, therefore, he looked up at the man from the country and became lost in thought - should he sign, or shouldn't he?

He paused so long that at last the man from the country became impatient. He snatched the paper from John Lang and said: "Well! Well! Take it - or leave it. Lots of men in your position would jump at such a chance. But, see here!" he said, holding out the paper once more, "I like the look of you, and I will stretch a point. I'm tired of the country - really sick of it."- and he almost shuddered as he said this. ("What an odd man!" thought John Lang.) "I'll give you a little money down on the transaction if that makes it easier. I see it looks as if I were getting the bird in hand, and you the bird in the bush, etc." And he laughed with his queer, short laugh.

"That's just it," said John Lang, laughing too. "That's just it."

"Well," said the man from the country, "here is my pocket-book. Look at it and take what you want out of that to make the bargain even. You see," he said, "there is money coming in at Greenleas; that's where this comes from." And he handed the pocket-book to John Lang.

This made a great difference, and John saw that there was plenty of money there, and that if he could repay himself for what he would lose by giving over his furniture, and take a little more to keep him going until he found a new place somewhere, if the place called Greenleas was a hoax, he would reduce his risk very much. And, oh, it was so tempting! Come what might, the dreariness of his present life would be cast off - and he would have some new experiences anyhow.

But he still hesitated. He took the agreement into his hand once more and read it over.

"By the way," he said, "what does Greenleas contain? I mean," he added, seeing that the man from the country looked very queer, "I mean, does it contain tables and chairs and cupboards, and all that kind of thing?"

"Oh yes. Plenty of them. See, here is a list of them. All the things I got when I took the house over. You can take this with you, you know."

John Lang took the book in which the lists were written and glanced through it, and saw that (everything was all right as far as that was concerned. "But," said he, "what do you mean exactly by speaking of the time when you 'took the house over?' Hasn't it always been yours?"

"No," said the man from the country.

"It has not always been mine. It came to me, you see."

"Oh! It came to you - I see. But how did it come to you? Did some relation leave it to you when he died?"

"No, no - there was no relation exactly. In fact, I did not exactly know him either."

"But how delighted you must have been to come into it!" said John Lang most cheerfully.

"I was. Yes - I was - very much delighted."

"Just one thing more. How about animals!" asked John Lang. "I do love animals! Are there animals at Greenleas?"

"Yes. Oh yes! Lots of creatures. There are lots of them - if you like them and all that sort of thing, you will be very happy."

"But you don't like them, I see," said John Lang.

The man from the country shrugged his shoulders at this remark, and again gave a sort of little shudder. But John Lang did not notice this, and once more got ready to sign the agreement. Yet once more he paused, and asked the stranger:

"I suppose one does not live by oneself at Greenleas?'

"No!" was the answer. "One does not live by oneself there. There is - always - someone there."

"A person who helps about the place, I suppose; keeps things right and so on?" asked John.

"Yes. That is the kind of thing," said the other. "You will soon see when you get there. There is someone there, and you can always get extra help if wanted."

"So I shall not be lonely. That's good," said John. "One reason why I dislike living in this place where I am now is because I am so lonely."

"No, no; you won't be lonely!" said the man.

This encouraged John Lang so much that he began to sign the agreement. But once more he stopped, and, looking up, he asked: "Does one see the full moon at Greenleas? I do so love the sight of the full moon, and I could not live happily anywhere if the moon was hidden from it."

The man from the country again seemed to shiver a little at this moment. He did not seem to share John Lang's love of the full, moon; but he hastened to assure John that every full moon from rise to set could be watched from Greenleas.

So at last John Lang was satisfied. He made another copy of the agreement, and called in the night-watchman to be witness. He signed his name; the witness signed too. John took one paper himself; and then very seriously, and very solemnly, he handed the other one to the stranger from the country.

This other one snatched the paper from his hand, and to John's astonishment shouted "Joy! joy!" and then, without a moment's pause, rushed out of the room, up the stairs, and away down the street! The noise of his footsteps grew more and more faint, till at last it died away in the distance; but John Lang stood still in the place where he was, and for some minutes did not move at all.

The fact was that when the man turned and ran out of the room John noticed, for the first time, for one thing, that the stranger's coat had evidently been torn right down the back from the collar to the skirt! And for another, that at the back of his head the hair had been cut away and was replaced by huge strips of sticking-plaster!

However, John was so full of the feeling of delight at his good-fortune that he felt it was absurd to stand there thinking and getting worried by such things as these. He felt that the joy shown by the stranger from the country was nothing to his own. What, after all, were a few strips more or less of plaster on someone else's head compared to the fact that he himself was going to enjoy the ownership of a real home! Full of satisfaction, he spent the rest of the night in happy dreams of nothing but country things, of full moons, and of every kind of beauty and comfort.

CHAPTER 2

THE ARRIVAL

THE journey by train to Greenleas seemed rather long, but at last it was over, and he was out of the station and in the midst of the lovely land where he was to make his new home. Round the corner of a hill, through a wood, over a bridge, and there lay Greenleas before him!

Just at first it was rather a shock to see that very extensive repairs were going on. They were evidently wanted badly, for a bit of the roof was off, and part of the actual wall of the house was fallen down. A nice - looking, cheerful boy, however, came running out to meet him, and hastened to explain that everything would soon be all right; he was only so sorry it had not all been finished and put straight before the gentleman arrived.

"I thought you might be coming today," he said. "But," he added, "I am so sorry, I don't know your name."

"John Lang is my name," replied that gentleman heartily; "and what is yours, pray?"

"Oh, mine?" said the boy. "Oh, to be sure - yes - your name is John Lang. Yes, well - mine is Johnnie Greenleas!"

"Good," said John Lang. "But do tell me at once what has been happening here? Is it an earthquake?"

"No. Not exactly an earthquake!" said the boy.

"Storm of wind, then?"

"No, not exactly a storm of wind," said the boy.

"What sort of storm was it, then? Temper, perhaps?"   ,

"Why, yes. Perhaps that is more like it," replied Johnnie, chuckling with laughter and looking at John Lang out of the corners of his eyes. "Have you seen much of the man who gave Greenleas to you?"

" No."

" Didn't he tell you anything?"

" No, except a few things I asked about. Why should he?"

The boy muttered something or other to the effect that perhaps the "least said was soonest mended" - "the less said the better" - and so on; and left on John Lang's mind the impression that the man from the country was rather a poor creature. Quite unable to understand him, and really caring much more for an there was to be seen than about the cause of the damage, which was evidently being put to rights very rapidly, John Lang proposed that they should go inside the house.

"Let's go inside," he said, and go through the lists of things I was to take over in there."

So indoors they went. But if, the house was looking wrecked and knocked about outside, it was in even a worse condition within! So many things were at sixes and sevens that John Lang for a moment felt quite discouraged.

However, he was a man of good business habits, and he began at once most methodically, right at the beginning of the list the man from the country had given to him.

"Where's the dinner-set?" asks he, opening the book.

"Oh!" says the boy brightly, " there's the dinner-set!" And he pointed to a heap of fragments which were crushed into one corner. John Lang's eyes opened widely.

"And the tea-set?" asked he.

"There is the tea-set," said the boy, and pointed to a jumble of broken china which was piled upon a crumpled tea-tray, which seemed to have come to grief at the same time as the splintered and broken kitchen table, which, wanting one leg, was leaning in an uncomfortable way against a half - broken-down wall.

"Pretty bad!" thought John. And, indeed, had not some of the rooms of the house most fortunately escaped the general ruin, he would have felt very angry with the man from the country. Some rooms were beautiful, but in others beds were broken, mattresses were ripped up, sheets were torn into shreds, and tables and chairs were broken into splinters. Awful havoc had been wrought by somebody!

But there was one consoling point, and that was that things were already being put to rights, and, for another, there upon the table in the library, which was one of the uninjured rooms, was a large purse stuffed with money! So after all the stranger had not been so very far wrong. Money would not fail him any way. With the purse in his pocket and the boy to show him the way John Lang set out cheerfully enough to the little town not far off, to buy china and other things to replace all that had been destroyed.

As they went along everyone they met turned to look at them, and some people seemed inclined to speak to John Lang. But the boy did not permit this, and hurried him along to the shops where he proved to be most useful. He knew exactly where to get everything, and exactly what to get. No one could cheat him, no one could make him buy anything except exactly what he wanted. So the shopping was soon finished, and back they went to Greenleas.

There seemed to be no other people besides Johnnie who actually lived at Greenleas, but he was a host in himself, really a capital fellow. He worked with such a will that he got through as much as ten ordinary people; and so busy did he keep the men he employed that in a wonderfully short time all broken fragments were gone and all repairs in the house finished. Indeed, within a week of John Lang's arrival no traces remained of the upset, and the workmen left him and Johnnie to carryon life together.

While the workmen were there the absence of any animals about the place did not actually surprise John Lang, though once or twice it occurred to him that, far from finding signs of plenty of animals, of dogs and horses and so on, at Greenleas, there was not even a cat to be seen! When the workmen were gone and the whole place was empty and quiet, except for their two selves, he did feel it very odd that Greenleas was in this way so very different from what he had been led to expect.

"Johnnie," he said, "where are all the animals belonging to this place?"

"Animals?" answered Johnnie. "Do you want them?"

"Why," said John Lang," of course I do!"

"Do you like them? Well, you will be very different from the other gentlemen - I mean gentleman," he said, looking at

John Lang in that queer way of his, out of the corners of his eyes. "Why, some people actually dislike animals!"

"But how? Dislike them?" exclaimed John Lang. "The man who gave all this over to me said they were like friends. No, he didn't exactly say that - ; but at any rate he said - or implied - that there were all sorts of beasts here. And I had hoped that they even came into the house! Now I should love that - at least, I should not mind. Do you think," he asked of the boy, who was still looking at him - "do you think that man ..... did anything to drive them away? Were they perhaps too friendly? What you might call too tame for taste?"

"I think," said the boy slowly- "I think he may have thought he did not want them quite so near him. Yes, yes - I think he did find them what you call 'too tame.'"

"Did you ever see him driving them away?" broke in John Lang.

"Yes," confessed the boy, "y - e - s. I did. I feel sure that he did - he wanted to drive them off."

"Brute!" said John Lang; then, seeing the boy begin to smile, he added: "And you helped him, I expect."

"Oh no, no - never, never. I would not think of such a thing. Never, never," he added again and again quite firmly."

"That's a comfort," said John Lang, now quite convinced by the boy's earnestness. "I have a dog coming tomorrow, and we must teach him at once not to chase away any creatures which come. For, you do think they will come again?" he asked rather anxiously.

"Oh yes," said the boy, now beaming with satisfaction. "I think you may depend upon it that they will come back. I think you may be quite - perfectly sure of that, at all events, if that is what you want. Quite sure - quite, quite sure. They always do come, you know," he added cheerfully, "at the proper time."

"I'm glad of that," said John Lang.

CHAPTER 3

THE COMING OF THE DOG

THE next morning the dog arrived, safe and well, a delightful rough terrier, with a wise head and pricked-up ears, all eager to see his new home and to be set free from the chain by which he was fastened to the carrier's cart in which he arrived.

"Want a dog!" said the carrier. "What, haven't you enough things here already round you?" Then very solemnly he put up his hand to his mouth and said right in John Lang's ear: "He'll be no use, you know."

"How do you mean 'no use'?" cried John Lang. "How do you mean? I want him for a friend, and to enjoy himself with me."

"Oh, to enjoy himself with you! Is that it?" said the man. "That's all right as far as it goes - till moon comes." And here he shook his head sagely. "Till moon comes," he repeated.

"Why, what do you mean?" cried John, quite puzzled. "What do you mean?"

The man looked at John Lang long and curiously, and, instead of answering his question, asked him back: "How long have you been here, sir?"

"Only a week," replied John; "but look here, just tell me, please, what you mean by 'till moon comes.'"

The man was just opening his mouth to answer when the voice of the boy broke in. "Hulloa, old Dawdles!" it cried, "much good you do stopping hours everywhere before you deliver anything at all!"

On hearing this voice the carrier, without waiting for the boy to come round the corner of the house, looked hurriedly up at the sky and muttering, " Goodness, there's Georgie!" jumped briskly into his cart, whipped up his horse, and went bumping off down the road without a word of explanation or of farewell.

John Lang would have at once spent some time in wondering over what had passed if his attention had not been vigorously attracted to the dog. For this animal was behaving in rather a curious way. He had at the first moment returned his new master's greeting in a most friendly way; he had wagged a cheerful tail, licked John's' hand, and frisked round his feet in a manner which was most promising. But when the boy's voice was heard, and still more when he advanced to the side of John Lang, there was a complete change "of behaviour. A sullen angry look came over the animal, his tail dropped, his ears went back, the hair on his neck rose up. Stiff all over, and standing on his tip-toes, the dog gave a low and angry growl, while he turned back his upper lip so as to show his white and gleaming teeth. As the boy advanced the dog retreated, till he came bump against the legs of his new master, who stood watching in silence, wondering what was going to happen. The dog was evidently furiously excited by the boy; but the boy was cheerfulness itself. "Oh ho!" he said, "it's that way, is it? Well, well, well! Never mind. Let's give him some food after his journey, and see what happens then."

"Perhaps it is water he wants after his journey," said John, and he stooped down to pat and to reassure the frightened and enraged dog. At the sound of his voice, and touch of his hand the animal at once resumed his friendly aspect. But so it went on all day. Towards John Lang all was friendliness; towards the boy all enmity and even fear. It was rather boring, but he could not worry- everything else was so very jolly. Everything he had longed for had come to him, and when he went to bed at night he fell into his first comfortable doze, with the dog lying curled up comfortably at his feet just as he had always pictured as quite perfection.

But in a few moments he woke with a jump. What did the carrier mean by what he said? Why did he talk of Georgie? And why - oh, why would not the dog make friends with the boy? It was some time before he really went to sleep - and even then the questions were not answered.

CHAPTER 4

THE STORM, AND WHAT THAT LED TO

JOHN LANG would have liked to spend some time in rummaging about in the rooms which had been undisturbed when he first arrived. But for one thing the fine weather drew him out of doors, and for another the boy Johnnie seemed to be quite clearly bent on everything being left as it was. So for a time John was content to give himself up to do what the boy wished.

But the fine weather did not remain unbroken; clouds came up, and it so happened that on the night of the new moon a heavy storm began, and it rained all day. Now seemed to be the time to explore all the rooms and to examine the pieces of old furniture, the cupboards and bureaus which stood in the rooms, and to see what they contained. But the boy was still against it.

Towards evening, as it was very chilly, he lighted a fire in the big high library which had been one of the rooms left uninjured before John Lang came to the house. Like all the rooms on the ground floor, it had wide and high windows, which went down to the ground, by which one could pass freely out and in from the garden which surrounded the house. You could not see the river from this room; but it had a charming view over the garden, to the picturesque old barn, and beyond it far over the country to the east. But tonight they drew the curtains, and the firelight soon danced cheerfully all over the room.

John Lang sat watching everything, and presently he said:

"That's a jolly looking old cabinet, Johnnie, which is covered all over with brass patterns. What's in it?"

"Books," said Johnnie "nothing else."

John Lang was getting up to examine further, when, seeing the halma-board spread out and Johnnie all eager for a game, he changed his mind and put away all thoughts of everything else for the moment.

What a delightful change all this friendly companionship was from his dismal and lonely life before the man from the country sent him down to Greenleas!

John himself won the first game, a very stiff battle. Then Johnnie won the second. So they piled up the fire and started on the conqueror game in high spirits.

"My goodness, what a storm is going on!" said John. "How comfortable it is in here!" And he turned his whole attention to the winning of the game.

Johnnie was a good player. But John Lang won, and when he had won few things could have pleased him better than the cheery way in which Johnnie took his beating. Johnnie was, it seemed, such a pleasant fellow to live with. It seemed more than ever queer that that nice terrier disliked him so.

They talked of this as they sat a little time over the fire after their games. Presently, however, they both grew sleepy and went off to bed.

Johnnie may have slept well; but John Lang, though he had been very sleepy when he went upstairs, could not get off to sleep at all. The fact is that he had a great deal to think about. As he was going upstairs he came past a big window which had no curtains, and stood for a moment looking out upon the sky. A great wind was blowing and huge clouds were rushing along with it. Now and then a break would come, and in one of these came a fleeting vision of the new moon, far away, but so distinct that you could feel you had only to put out your hand and touch it, and see for yourself what it was made of.

"Ah!" John cried, "there's the moon - how jolly!" And in a moment the carriers' words, "Till the moon comes," jumped into his mind. What did the carrier mean? He looked at Johnnie and found that the boy was, even while he stifled a yawn, watching him with that queer sideways look of his.

"Tut! Tut!" said John Lang out loud, and to himself he said:

"What does it matter what he meant? I shall soon know, I expect."

These were wise thoughts - but the storm raged; trees were snapping in the wind, windows and doors were shaking and clattering. It was of no use to go on trying to get off to sleep. So at last John Lang took his candle and went downstairs, determined to get a book out of the old cabinet, so as to read for a bit and not bother about the moon. He threw open the cabinet doors and pulled out book after book from the shelf which was revealed inside. It was a great bore, but like so many books none of them seemed as interesting inside as they looked on the outside, and he grew more and more disappointed as he piled them one after another upon a sort of convenient bracket, which stuck out on one of the cabinet's inside walls, so as to make sure that he had examined them all. He had got a good way through the lot, and was beginning to think he would find nothing at all to his mind, when just as he was laying one down he was astonished to hear a loud click! And then at the back of the bookshelf from which he had taken the books a small door sprang open in his face, and he was surprised to see that there was a lovely secret hiding-place within. This was most exciting. What would he find here!

CHAPTER 5

THOSE BOOKS

THE little cupboard within the big cabinet which had sprung open when John Lang had piled books upon the bracket to one side of him was, he found, altogether the cleverest thing of the sort which could possibly be imagined. It was so contrived that just so much weight as he happened to have put upon it (no more and no less, for he often tried afterwards) would undo the hidden fastening. The secret of how to open the hiding-place was not easy to discover. But here it was, and by chance, discovered by John Lang himself. And now - was there anything in that secret hiding-place? Yes, indeed! There was just room inside it for two more books, evidently very precious books, or they, would have been outside with the others. They were not large, but evidently they were very old.

John Lang eagerly opened first one and then the other, but he found that at first sight they also were strangely disappointing. One of them, which was old, but less old than the other, was a well-filled notebook, which contained many pages of accounts, and pages given up to calculations about eclipses and changes of the moon. The other, and older book of the two, seemed at first sight to be filled to a large extent with pages which appeared to be quite blank!

John Lang was inclined to throw the two books back into their hiding-place and go back to bed without books at all, when his eye was caught by an admirable picture of Greenleas, and, a few pages further on, one of the boy Johnnie!

These pictures were in the book which was partly full of pages on which nothing was to be seen. Turning over another page, he found an elaborate plan of the ground-floor of the house, with its surroundings and outhouses. This looked much more promising. So he stuffed both the old books in his pocket, shut the secret recess, put the other books back in front of it, and hied off back to his bedroom.

It was very chilly, and he was glad when he was safely and comfortably tucked up in bed again.

When safely there he opened first one and then the other of his treasures. There was the picture of the house. And there, on another page, Was the likeness of the boy. Only the figure, which was drawn so carefully in pen and ink, was in totally different clothes to those of the present day. So this picture must be, John Lang said to himself, of some ancestor of the boy, and not actually of the boy himself as he had at first supposed. Yet it was curiously like the present boy. Though the clothes were so queer, and though there was a queer, collar round the neck, the face which looked out over the collar was the face of Johnnie, and it had on it that odd sideways look which was so remarkable in the young fellow who had looked at John Lang when they had watched the new moon out of the window together.

Many blank pages came after this portrait, and then, further on, the plan of the house and surroundings; and then more blank pages, and presently another picture of the house as seen by the light of the full moon.

This might have been very pretty, but it was quite spoilt, John Lang thought, by the artist having put into this picture another portrait of that person like Johnnie. But the absurd thing was that the figure was drawn so huge that the house looked small beside it.

That was all, except a page full of pictures of beasts very badly drawn, and without any names or explanations. The whole thing was tantalizing and puzzling, for as far as he could make out there was exceedingly little actually written in the book, Here and there were a few words, and a few sentences; and, curiously enough, these words and sentences were all of a kind to make you long for more. "Then" stood all by itself. On another page was "Alas!" and nothing else at all. "Beware" was on another page, and neither that word nor the warning "Mind now," nor the single word "If," had any connecting-links with any other part of the book. Still more maddening was it to read in one page" Never allow yourself," and on another "What ever happens, don't," and not to be told what" you," who ever that was, were not to "allow" yourself ; nor what it was that you should avoid! There was nothing else. Nothing at all but the pictures and those few words among all the pages of the book. Everything else was blank.

It was very provoking, and having laid the book upon the table beside him, John Lang took up the other one, which contained the notes and the accounts. Hardly anything at all in this book could interest John Lang tonight. It was not as old as the other book, but the other one, at all events, made you think. In this book page after page was full of uninteresting dates - days of the month chiefly, without mention of the year. Those pages which referred to the eclipses and changes of the moon were mixed up with the names of beasts of various kinds - Centaur, Hellephant, rat and others, no reason at all being given why they were noted down - and besides these, pages and pages of accounts. "Boots for Willie" so much; "stockings for Willie" so much - all over and over again, and more and more expensive each time. Then came expenditure on food, and once the note "£26 all in one week - my money is nearly gone." Altogether it seemed to be a dull and dismal book, utterly silly and useless for him, John Lang thought; and, seeing that his candle was burning very low, and being himself surprised by the necessity for a violent sneezing fit, he blew out the light, pulled the bedclothes up nearly over his head, and presently, in a lull in the storm, went fast asleep.

CHAPTER 6

MORE ABOUT THOSE BOOKS, AND SOMETHING ABOUT A COLD

IN the morning after the storm John Lang awoke with a very bad cold. But striking and boring as this would have been in ordinary circumstances, it did not strike him at first. What did strike him, and that very strongly, was that the boy was standing by his bedside staring from one to the other of the two ancient books which had come from the hiding-place. One of them - the one with the accounts - was in his hand, the other was lying open - on the table. The dog, who, as usual, was sleeping on John Lang's bed, was pressing himself back against the wall and snarling at the boy in his usual fashion. But the boy was paying no attention to the dog, and it was the expression of his face which so occupied John Lang's mind that at first he neither moved nor spoke. The boy was evidently intensely thrilled by the sight of the books, and he turned from one to the other of them with an impatient hurry and look of intense eagerness which was most interesting to watch.

At last John Lang put out his hand and touched the boy, and asked him quietly: "Well? What's wrong?"

The boy started, laid down the book hurriedly, and stammering and confused said: "You have had a bad night, sir? Goodness me!" he added, "what a cold you have caught! I must light a fire here. You must not get up today."

Indeed, a violent coughing fit laid hold of poor John Lang, who saw plainly enough that the lovely day which had succeeded the wild storm of the previous night was not to be enjoyed by him. He must nurse his tiresome cold. Yes, a fire must be lighted, and he must be cured as quickly as was possible.

So a fire was lighted. And then Johnnie, brisk and cheerful once more, proceeded to dust and to put the room all straight. But for once Johnnie was clumsy - he knocked down several things, he upset a chair, he tipped over the jug of water, and finally, with a huge clatter, by a clumsy movement while he was sweeping the floor, he overturned the table upon which lay the two ancient books.

As ill-luck would have it, Johnnie had stood the table, while he was sweeping, close to the fire, so that when the upset came they fell right into the flames.

Johnnie, with a loud expression of dismay, stood spell-bound, looking at what he had done, wringing his hands and saying: "Oh, they are burning! They are burning!"

John Lang was furiously angry, of course, and leaping out of bed, he snatched the treasures out of the flames. Too late to save the notebook, alas! - that was, in the instant, a hopelessly flaming mass of paper. But the other book - the one with the pictures - he did save in great measure; for though many of the edges of most of the pages were blackened, only one page was on fire, and quite spoilt, before John Lang could put it out by pressing it under the hearth-rug. That this one page happened to contain the curious portrait which was so like Johnnie was most annoying. John Lang was exceedingly vexed, and was very cross all day with Johnnie. The boy, however, never relaxed his attentions: and as he seemed to have mastered his clumsiness of the morning, and proved himself a kind and attentive fellow, doing all he could to make his cold - afflicted master comfortable, John Lang presently felt he had to forgive him. He really had an exceedingly bad cold, and was glad of Johnnie's ardent ministrations.

CHAPTER 7

THE DOCTOR AND THE CUPBOARD

AND so the days passed on. And the moon, which had been "new" at the time of the storm, grew larger and larger each night, and John Lang felt sure he would be well enough by the time it was "full" to enjoy the beauty of it to the uttermost. It was wonderful how much he felt drawn towards the thoughts of the growth of the moon. He supposed it was because he had so little to do just now, and because he had seen so much about it in the book which was so unfortunately burnt. The time of the full moon seemed something to look forward to while he was getting rid of his tiresome cold.

The doctor had been to see John Lang. Johnnie had rather ridiculed the idea of sending for him, but John Lang had insisted because he so much wanted to get quite well again quickly. When the doctor came, I am sorry to say, Johnnie did not behave at all well. John Lang was once more quite displeased with him. He would not leave them alone together for one minute. His master had hoped to get some information from the doctor about the former inhabitants of Greenleas. But Johnnie kept breaking into the room with all sorts of pretexts which quite prevented his opening the subject. Imagine it! Once he burst into the room shouting: "The butcher has called - does the doctor say you may eat beef?" Then another time he burst in with: "The grocer is here - is raspberry jam good for you?" Then: "Oh, I say! The fish hasn't come!" Then: "Oh, I say! I'm afraid the boiler is going to burst!" This last intrusion came just as John Lang was showing the doctor the ancient book which remained. He angrily ordered Johnnie to go, and not come back. But not three minutes had passed before the boy's voice was heard outside the door saying humbly: "Please, sir, doctor's wanted - in a great hurry." And after that, of course, there was no more hope. The doctor was out of the room and off like a shot.

When he paid his second visit John Lang was up and out in the garden, and the good doctor only put his head over the garden hedge to shout congratulations without getting off his horse. So from him John got no information at all about the former history of the house and of the people who had lived in it. But while he had been getting better he had found out a certain number of things for himself, for as soon as he was out of his own room again he continued his examination of cupboards and wardrobes. In one of the latter he came upon a certain bundle of things which was thrust out of sight, behind several ancient quilts, which were found, when they were unrolled, to be almost tumbling to pieces with moth.

The moths, however, had not reached the bundle behind the quilts, and when this was opened, it was found to contain a suit of clothes such as had been worn by men of about a hundred years ago, but of such huge size that they seemed to have been made for a veritable giant.

When John Lang unrolled the bundle Johnnie, who was standing just behind him, gave a sort of gasp! "Oh! Oh!" he cried, "that's where they are - so he never - " Here he stopped, and, seeing that John Lang was looking at him questioningly, he held out his hands to take the things, and tried to carry off the awkwardness of the situation by shaking them out and refolding them.

"Have you ever 'seen these things before?" asked John Lang with the utmost kindness, for he felt that something had upset Johnnie.

"Well!" cried Johnnie in a shaky voice. "Well-ye-I mean-I've heard of them."

"Heard of them! From whom? And what did you hear?"

"Oh, don't ask me," said Johnnie, shivering - "don't please ask me. Oh, don't - it can come to no good!"

"No good - how do you mean, then? No good to you? or no good to me?"

"To me," cried Johnnie, "to me! and to you! Oh, don't ask me!". And the boy began to look so queer, and so very, very cross that John Lang for the moment changed the subject, and told Johnnie to give him down the things which were upon the shelf above the one where the bundle of clothes had been stowed. Johnnie obeyed with alacrity, and reached up as if he expected to do as he was asked with perfect ease. But, as it happened, his arms were several inches short of what he aimed at. A look of great anger came over his face then.

"Sold!" he muttered, "sold! I meant to have looked there, and now it's too soon."

"Too soon?" asked John Lang, puzzled again - "too soon for what?"

The boy now burst into a hearty laugh. Throwing away his anger, he said with merry chuckles: "Oh, I'll be growing soon, and then I can reach you everything you want. It's growing! It's growing! When it's big I shall grow!"

So merry was his laugh, so pleasant was the change from his anger, that John Lang, who could not bear to see people look anything but happy, laughed too, though he still felt very much puzzled. What was the "it" which was "growing"? What could Johnnie mean by "It's growing"? and then the thought of the moon slipped into his mind. "Tut, tut!" said he to himself, "why am I always thinking about the moon?"

But it was luncheon time now. So, leaving the clothes upon the floor in a heap, John Lang went downstairs, saying to Johnnie as he went that the old quilts must certainly be burnt, or they would be spreading moth all over the house.

While he was eating his luncheon he smelt the burning, and was pleased with the promptitude with which his wishes had been carried out. He was not long in finishing his lunch, for he was keen to get back to the upstairs room, and to examine the clothes he had found. He thought it very probable that in the pockets of the clothes, of which there seemed to be many, he might find some clue to the history of their owners, and of the old books which left him. so puzzled. Perhaps those huge clothes had belonged to that "Willie" whose boots and other things had been so perplexingly expensive. You ca n then imagine how dreadfully disappointed he was when he found that Johnnie had made a bonfire not only of the quilts, but also of the suit of clothes! Not only had he done this, but he had fetched some steps, had cleared all the things from the upper shelf, had burnt them too, and was now busily engaged, standing on the high steps to do it, in scrubbing out the wardrobe.

"Really, Johnnie, you are too active!" cried John Lang in anger. "I wanted those old clothes. Do you realize Willie might have - " But he never finished the sentence, for, with a sharp crash, the shelf came clattering to the ground, and Johnnie was left in a precarious position on top of the steps, which were only just poised by one corner against the cupboard door.

Some papers fell out from behind the shelf, and catching sight of the names "George" and "Georgy" upon one of them, John Lang stopped his sentence abruptly and swooped down to pick up the precious document. But as he stooped the crash came, and down upon his bent back came the steps, and Johnnie, and the pail of water, and the soap, and the scrubbing-brush, all in one heavy and most wetting confusion. For a. few moments there was upon the ground a very uncomfortable heap, and when John and Johnnie regained their feet and wiped the soapy water from their eyes and hair, the papers were all crumpled - all soaked and destroyed. They were past all possible use, and utterly defaced. Of course, John Lang was angry, but being angry did not restore what was lost! Much was lost, but he could not, however, fail to reckon up what he had gained too. For one thing, he had seen the clothes, and for another, he had gained another mention of the name of "Georgie" which had been used by the carrier. When so much was puzzling even an increase to the puzzle might help to solution.

What a pity that huge suit of clothes had been destroyed! What if, by careful comparison of them with those worn by the figure in that picture in which the house was made to look so small, he could have been decided that there was once a real giant at Greenleas? And the giant's name might have been discovered too! However, time would show. It was most interesting.

CHAPTER 8

THE FIRST FULL MOON

AND here at last comes the time to which John Lang has looked forward so much. Here at last comes the date of his first full moon at Greenleas.

It had been a lovely day, cloudless and perfectly bright. But the sunset and moonrise were hazy, and before long there were a good many clouds over the sky. It was exceedingly provoking. The full roundness of the moon was, it seemed, to be denied him. The rays of that full moon were to be stuck fast in the big cloud-cushions and to be hidden from John Lang.

This made him really quite sulky, and he felt inclined to lose his temper badly. He was all the more aggravated because the boy, after having been rather timid and retiring since the day when the old clothes were found and burnt, seemed to be regaining his' spirits almost too fast. He was more like what he had been on the day of the doctor's visit, when he had made conversation with that gentleman impossible. He frisked about, he made faces at the snarling dog. He even threw his boots clattering down the stairs when he was undressing, and John Lang could hear him shouting a sort of song at the top of his voice -

"Mi-se-rable lit-tle things!
Lit-tle sil-ly ti-ny things-"

in a high piercing voice which came ringing through the house in a way John Lang felt to be most disagreeable. So the owner of Greenleas was not quite as happy as usual when he went to bed, and his vexation was not lessened by the sound of a rat scurrying away when he opened his bedroom door. Fancy his disgust when (having given up all hopes of watching the full moon, he had just fallen asleep) he was awakened by the noise of that rat once more racqueting about all over the room.

"Shoo!" he said, "shoo! Get away, you beast!" But it did not get away, so he lighted a candle and tried to make the dog get down from the foot of the bed to help him with the rat hunt.

The dog had been annoying before; but now he seemed simply to have gone silly. He entirely refused to help John Lang in any way whatever.

"Frightened by a rat, you utterly foolish and futile animal!" cried John. "If you won't chase a rat, you shall not lie warm and lazy on my bed. Out you go!" And he flung open the door. The dog took him at his word. With his tail between his legs and with every sign of abject terror, and, with all his hair standing on end, he rushed downstairs, along the furthest possible passage, and took refuge in the deepest and darkest recess of the boot-hole! He preferred the barest of boards alone, to warm blankets in proximity to the rat!

"Why, the poor thing is moonstruck," cried John, for he had been so comic, really, in his rush that his master was driven to laughter, and got into bed again quite chuckling with amusement, and hoped now that he would get good sound sleep.

But no such luck was to be his. There was the rat again!

He shouted at it. He threw things at the places where he heard it. Time after time he thought it was gone, time after time it returned. Every now and then when he had been: chasing it he would draw back the curtain to see if the moon was shining, and once he saw it between the clouds, full and round. After this he dozed a bit, thinking the rat was quite gone now. But again no! There it was once more, only a very few minutes after the light was put out, and this time it was upon the table by the bedside, with two glowing red eyes, and it was nibbling, nibbling away at something it found there which was evidently good to eat! This was a quiet amusement, at all events, and for a short time John Lang lay quiet too. Then it struck him all of a heap-" What was the rat eating?" There was no food upon the table, nothing but a box of matches! The candles were upon the chimney-piece. But, the book! That was it!

In horrid fear that his precious book would be spoilt, John seized the matches and got a light. The rat, of course, jumped off the table in an instant; but it was evident that it was the book it had been nibbling at, for in many places it had bitten right into the leaves and left the marks of its teeth all along the edges of almost all of them.

This was too much, and placing the lighted candle upon the table and the book under his pillow, and' arming himself with a heavy football boot, John Lang lay down to await events.

On the top of a bookcase at one side of the room was a beautiful and valuable old clock which John had brought from one of the lower rooms because he liked to hear its quiet companionable ticking, and to see exactly whether the boy was punctual in the mornings or not. The boy had laughingly protested, and said that he was always punctual. Which indeed, he proved to be. But it was exactly on the top of this clock, and right over the middle of its face, that the rat appeared next. John had not quite closed the curtain when he had looked out last, and it so happened that at the very last moments before its setting the moon shone out clear and bright from among the clouds; and by its light, though now lessened in glory by the approach of sunrise, John Lang saw the wicked rat. He saw it clearly, sitting up, looking straight at him with its red eyes, and - surely it could not be true? And yet he felt sure of it - that rat grinned at him!

It squeaked, too, as if in defiance and to say: "You cannot get me here!"

"I will get you, though!" shouted John Lang, and he hurled his boot with violence straight at the clock-face and the rat. There was a crash and a splintering of glass, and then silence.

The sun rose while the full moon set, and a new day's light began. The clock-face was smashed - that was sad. But presumably the rat was smashed too - that was a comfort. Anyway, it came no more for the present, and perhaps it would come no more at all. Perhaps John could snatch a wink of sleep now before he was called, and this he did very soundly on the whole, though still restlessly and with a good many dreams of strange and perplexing things, which somehow he could neither understand nor get explained to him. So that he was glad when he heard the boy stirring and coming to his room to open the curtains wide and let in the full daylight.

CHAPTER 9

CHANGE

SO the morning came, and with it the boy Johnnie. Contrary to his usual tidy habits, he came in in his stocking-feet only.

"Take care!" shouted John Lang. "What are you doing without your boots? There is no need to be so very quiet as all that. Go and get your boots, or put on my slippers. Mind you don't get any glass into your feet!"

He lay back again sleepily on his pillow, watching the boy with half-closed eyes. Then it struck him how very quickly boys do grow - for there was no doubt about it, the boy's trousers seemed to be getting very short for him; so short did they look that John Lang wondered he had never noticed it before. The boy was meanwhile sweeping up the pieces of the clock-face, and examining the whole thing very carefully.

"Not much harm done this time," he said to himself. And to his master: "Only the glass broken after all - that can soon be put right;" and he turned and left, the room.

As he left John Lang, watching him still, thought he had not noticed before that the boy's head came so high as it now did against the door-frame. "How fast boys do grow!" he thought, as he shook himself together and began to get up.

The thought of Johnnie's height did not occupy him long. He was in a hurry to get up, and to go downstairs and out of doors, to shake off the feeling of the discomfort of his disturbed night. The worry of it still hung about him. He felt as if somehow he had been through some very unusual experience.

"And yet I have only had a rat in my room," he said to himself; and he reminded himself how very often this had happened before in his cellar-room at the factory. And he scolded himself for being so quickly softened by comfortable things that so very little could upset him so much.

He shook himself; but though he might feel more brisk all over for doing this, he could not quite shake off the memory of the way that rat had sat up in the moonlight and had grinned at him as it sat upon the clock. He even spoke of it to the boy.

"Dreams," said that person - "dreams. George used to dream."

"George?" asked John Lang, jumping at the name. "What do you know about George?"

CHAPTER 10

JOHNNIE'S NEW CLOTHES

TO this question, "What do you know about George?" Johnnie answered very little, but just stood there looking at John Lang out of the corners of his eyes in his funny way.

John was really angry now, and was insisting on an answer to his question, when there came a sudden noise of tearing and of ripping of cloth - as if someone's clothes were all coming to pieces with violence! What was happening?

Why, simply that! The boy's clothes had all burst at the seams with violence and were coming to pieces, and were falling off him in strips, while the buttons were flying all over the place. One of them actually hit John Lang in the eye. It was most unpleasant. "Tut, tut!" said Johnnie, "I'm afraid you will be annoyed!"

"Annoyed?" cried John, mopping his injured eye - " annoyed?" The word seemed to him to be hardly strong enough.

"But," said the boy, "what are you going to do?"

"Do?" shouted John Lang - "do?" Again the word did not please him.

"Yes, do," said Johnnie. "I can't go about like this."

"No, indeed!" That was quite evident, but John Lang did not in the least know what he or anyone could "do" under such circumstances.

But Johnnie knew, and, indeed, had his plan quite ready. He must, he said, for the moment, wear a suit of John Lang's clothes, and they must then go down to the tailor's, that he might be measured for some new clothes of his own.

"And we may as well take the clock to be mended at the same time, and then that will be done," said Johnnie.

The dog utterly declined to leave his refuge. So John Lang determined to stop on their way at the station, and Ito send off a telegram to the man from whom he had bought the animal, insisting on a change. "For," said he, "such a coward of a dog is no use."

As he said this, the remembrance of what the carrier had said flashed upon his mind - "It won't be any use!" and "It's all right as far as it goes," and "Till the moon comes." Certainly the moon did seem to have upset the poor dog a good deal - or was it the rat which was to blame? Perhaps this dog was particularly liable to be upset by moons. The full moon does (as John Lang very well knew) often make dogs want to sit outdoors and howl. But, anyway, John did not want a dog who was afraid of rats, or of moons or of anything. It was best to make a change at once, especially as this dog was so stupid about Johnnie.

So John Lang and the great tall boy Johnnie set out cheerfully enough, and they came to die telegraph-office. While John Lang wrote out the telegram and handed it to the clerk Johnnie leant with both his elbows upon the counter, with an air of utter indifference, and looked as if his thoughts were far away. All went on as is usual on these occasions until the clerk had counted the words of the telegram and opened his drawer to take out the necessary stamps. As he did so, however, he said in a cheerful and confiding way to John Lang:

"Parting with your dog already, I see, sir?"

Johnnie gave a little start, and looked from one to the other of the two with that sidelong glance of his, which looked more than ordinarily quaint above John Lang's collar, tie, and coat, which matched so much better with John Lang than with their present wearer.

"How do you mean 'already?'" asked John Lang, who saw a possible chance for some useful knowledge from this outsider. "How do you mean' already?' "

"Why," the clerk began slowly as he tore off the stamps," the last man, you see - " But his sentence was never ended, because Johnnie, officiously stretching out his hand for the stamps, overturned a full ink-bottle right among all the office papers which were upon the counter.

A storm of abuse followed, profuse apologies from John Lang, great confusion, some anxiety, and finally a considerable payment by that gentleman for damage done to public property, and for the stamps which were spoilt. It was a horrid bore, and it was not until some time afterwards that the unfinished answer of the telegraph clerk returned to John Lang's mind, and when it did return to him so many and much more important things were in his head that this matter seemed quite small. What these things were we shall see later. For the present we must follow our two friends to the tailor's shop where Johnnie was to be measured for new clothes.

As they came near, to the tailor's shop it became evident that things were taking place there. The shop front was being painted, and there was a little delay about getting in at the door while a painter's ladder was being moved.

"Very sorry, sir," said the painter. "The old man's son has come from London to help him, and things are being smartened up a bit."

"Is the old man going away?" asked Johnnie.

"Not he," said the painter. "He knows too much about the customers;" and then he looked Johnnie all up and down and said: "Now, you, for instance .... "

"Here, hurry up," said Johnnie very rudely.

"We have something better to do than stand about all day;" and he pushed past the painter and held open the shop door for John Lang.

Then our two got into the small shop, and the young girl who was standing there asked their names. "For," said she, "I and my father are not familiar with things as yet."

"Mr. John Lang from Greenleas," replied that gentleman. "I want some new clothes for my servant here."

"I'll tell my father," said she; "he's in there with grandfather."

Out bustled Mr. Smith junior in answer to the summons. He took the measurements and the girl wrote them down; but they were interrupted by the questions of the old man within.

"Is that Georgie again?" asked the querulous old voice.

No answer.

"I say! Is that George?"

"No, father, no," said Mr. Smith junior.

"Excuse me, sir, I'm a newcomer, and it is my father who knows everyone. He likes to know who is in the shop. Excuse me, I think the name is Mr. John Lang of Greenleas?"

"Yes, it is, and this boy's name is Johnnie - Johnnie Greenleas."

"It's Johnnie Greenleas, father, whom I am measuring," shouted Mr. Smith junior to the invisible old gentleman.

"Johnnie? Johnnie?" murmured the aged voice within. "New that is. Georgie, now - I know Georgie," it chuckled, "and Willie, now - I know Willie. And I've heard tell of Tommie - yes, and Harry. But Johnnie, now, I wonder how that is?"

"Mary," burst in Mr. Smith junior, who had been growing redder and redder with vexation at these interruptions, "go in and quiet your grandfather. I'll put down the measurements myself." And so the matter ended; but it cannot be said that the puzzle was growing any more clear to John Lang. And what happened as they went home did not enlighten him either.

As they went back through the streets of the little town it annoyed our already irritated gentleman to be waylaid by first one man and then another offering help in all sorts of directions. First the man from the china shop pounced upon him to ask if there were any orders this morning. The clockmaker said he would gladly come over to Greenleas at any time to do repairs. The manager of the furniture shop came running out to say he had every kind of carpet and curtain ready in stock, and would charge nothing for laying down carpets nor for measuring the rooms - "in fact," he said, "I have most of the measures already, sir, at any time you may want me."

John Lang was really grateful now to Johnnie, at whose frown these fussy people retired one after the other with profuse apologies. John was a shy man himself and could not bear to refuse kind offers, even of things he did not want, but it needed all Johnnie's charms and fun to coax his master out of the state of worry into which he fell.

However, the weather was gorgeous; Johnnie was cheerful; the fishing was excellent; and no one - least of all a courageous and patient person such as John Lang - could resist the peaceful happiness which poured in upon him.

CHAPTER 11

THE NEXT FULL MOON

THE new dog arrived, a fine mastiff, and John Lang was delighted with its beauty and its wonderful friendly gentleness. It was too big to live in the house, and so it was taken to a large and comfortable kennel which stood by the backdoor. So charming was the animal that John Lang was the more annoyed when he found that, at the sight of cheerful and merry Johnnie, this new and powerful animal behaved in exactly the same way as the poor frightened terrier.

Nothing would induce the animal to come out of the depths of his kennel when Johnnie was near him. John Lang tried the plan of letting Johnnie alone give him food, hoping to teach him to love the person who produced it. But when, driven by hunger, the good animal ate a meal prepared and left for him by Johnnie, he was violently sick, though food prepared by John Lang himself was readily taken and thoroughly enjoyed.

The fuss went on for a whole ten days, and then John Lang felt it was no use to go on any longer wasting the lovely weather in coaxing dogs, however charming they might be. And so the mastiff followed the terrier back to London, and for a time Greenleas was again without any animals.

But it did not seem as if the place was to be without any animals at all, for on the night of the next full moon something curious happened.

Since the night when the rat had made its supper off part of the curious old book, John Lang had, as a rule, slept with the ancient book under his pillow, and by day he had carried it about with him in an inner pocket of his coat, so that it should be quite safe. Tonight, however (not noticing anything odd in the room), he allowed Johnnie to fold up his clothes as he took them off; and Johnnie was so full of fun and merriment, that John quite forgot to remove the book from his pocket and to stow it away under his pillow. He remembered it just as he was going off to sleep; but as there had been no rats about for the last four weeks, he thought he would not bother to fetch it. He had seen Johnnie folding up the coat, and there it was all right; he would turn over and go to sleep.

But he did not sleep for long. There was an odd noise in the room which woke him up. He had drawn back the curtains before he went to bed so that he should get full benefit of the bright moonlight when it came to where it could shine in at his window. Imagine his surprise when he saw that the noise was made by a funny, merry little Imp which had come into his room and was dancing about all over the place coat in hand, shaking it up and down, and now pouncing upon the book as it fell to the floor! The imp was a thin, mischevious, little figure with red skin and pointed ears.

Of course, John Lang dashed out of bed and after the mischievous creature. But before he could get to it the Imp was tearing the precious thing all to pieces and scattering them out of the window to the wind. John Lang got hold of the cover and a few of the leaves only - the rest were gone. The wind was arching them, and driving them, some into the cabbage-bed, and some far away into the river. It was too bad! A regular bad fate seemed to hang over that ancient book.

There was not time to be sorry though. That sprightly, grinning little Imp must be caught and must be prevented from doing any more harm. Very easy to think this, very easy indeed to say it! But how to do it? That was the point. In vain John Lang dashed and jumped from one side of the room to the other. The Imp dashed and jumped far better than he did. Over the bed, under the bed, backwards and forwards, among the legs of the chairs, onto the wardrobe and off again went the Imp, and John Lang after it, shouting all the time at the top of his voice for Johnnie to come and help him. At last (as John Lang sank for a breathless moment on to the side of one of the overturned chairs) it looked as if the Imp was going to stay still enough te let itself be caught; for it perched itself with an air of complete comfort on the handle of the water-jug, and sat there, and grinned at John. Now, it seemed, the moment for decisive action had really come. John Lang sprang to his feet, seized the chair, and with all his might hurled it at the tiresome little beast.

Crash went everything upon the wash-stand! Crash went the picture above it! And the Imp was gone! Gone clean out of the window, which John Lang very promptly shut firmly enough, so as to prevent its coming back again. Then he went to see why that vigorous and clever person Johnnie had not come to his help. But Johnnie's door was locked; and, by the sounds of snoring which came from within, John Lang was told that his friendly young servant was fast asleep after the labours of the day:

"Well, he does work very hard," thought John Lang (shrugging his shoulders as he went back to his own room), "if the noise the Imp and I have been making did not wake him up, nothing that I can do now will be any use. I must wait till morning to tell him all about it."

But when morning came John Lang forgot to tell about the Imp because of something which happened in the early dawn.

What that something was the next chapter will tell.

CHAPTER 12

PERPLEXITIES AND TROUBLES

WHAT happened was, that suddenly, from the room in which Johnnie was sleeping, came a great noise of the falling and breaking of wood.

Now, you must know that the bedsteads at Greenleas were many of them made, not of iron or brass, but of carved oak, with pillars and wooden tops to them, such as may be seen in the Victoria and Albert Museum. The one in the room occupied by Johnnie was especially beautiful and curious, and must have been very old and very valuable. But when John Lang rushed from his own room to Johnnie's to see what was happening, he found that during the night Johnnie had made a still more astounding jump in size than he had a month ago, and that his growth had been so vigorous that he had become too big and too heavy for his bed; and, there lay the poor beautiful thing all smashed to pieces!

So here was more trouble! Johnnie again far too big for his clothes, washstand smashed, bed broken to pieces. John Lang began to feel quite anxious about money affairs. For not only were there new things to buy, but Johnnie's appetite had increased with his size! And those words, "Twenty-six pounds! all in one week," which he had read in the old account-book, came back to his mind afresh. Whoever wrote those words knew something of the same kind of anxiety. And it was not altogether with a cheerful heart that he ordered new things to supply the places of those which were destroyed, and paid the bill for Johnnie's now enormous boots.

However, the rents of some farms were paid in just now, and the days went on and John Lang still felt that, in spite of all the queer things which were happening, there was nothing which would induce him to leave lovely Greenleas and to go back to his former life.

He went on feeling like that, although Johnnie's huge size was a perpetual reminder of how queer things were. It was not as if his size was any good. Johnnie was no good at all when a Twolf, a wolf with two heads, dashed into the larder at the next full moon, ate everything that was there, and broke a lot of dishes and plates. He grew that month, too, and was still no use. But, after all, the Twolf was not as annoying, really, as the next beast that came. Every moon brought a bigger beast than the one before; so John Lang did particularly dislike it when one lovely summer evening (as he was sitting on the terrace, watching the last glow of the sunset changing into the oncoming of moonlight) a large Lady Minotaur came slowly across the lawn swinging her tail from side to side.

The Lady Minotaur is the opposite of a Minotaur, which has a man's body and bull's head. This had a lady's head with small horns and a cow's body. She came along just as if she had a distinct plan in her mind. And though John stood in her way, waved his arms and shouted "Shoo!" very loud, the persistent beast avoided him with perfect calm and marched gravely on, John dancing in front of her, and still shouting things at her, and getting more and more angry. She dodged him cleverly and plunged up the steps of the terrace, and in at the open window. Through the open door of the room within she went, straight across the staircase hall to his mackintosh coat which was hanging on its hook in the front hall. This she proceeded to eat, drawing a piece of the skirt of it into her mouth with her clever tongue, munching it as if it were absolutely delicious.

So overcome with surprise was John by this queer proceeding that for a time he could do nothing. He had heard of a cow which ate things which were hanging to dry on hedges; he had never imagined anything like this! Indeed, it was some minutes before he got the coat away from her. He did this at length, and began in his fussed and bothered state to beat the Lady Minotaur over the head with what was left of the mackintosh. But far from annoying the Lady Minotaur, this conduct seemed to make it even more placid than before. Do what he could John could not prevent the heavy beast from turning back and lying down with a sigh of contentment on the floor of the staircase hall, and beginning slowly to chew the cud as if nothing out of the way were happening.

Would not you be annoyed at such doings? Well, John Lang was annoyed. But what would you have felt when, however you tried to push at the Lady Minotaur, however you tried to drag it by the horns, it just sat where it was and grinned. Think of this, and that it went on and on just chewing the cud, and grinning!

John Lang went to bed at last and left it there, but he could not help getting up from time to time and going to peep over the banisters to see if it was gone. Time after time he did this, feeling all the while an intense longing for the departure of that heavy dull presence. At last he felt a mysterious on - coming of relief - there was a feeling of change. He once more sprang out of bed and hurried to his post of observation on the top of the stairs.

What was it? Was it a sound? or a feeling? Something was surely going to happen? Yes, indeed! It was dawn which had come. And slowly, slowly, the light of the moon grew dim. As the moon slipped down out of sight and the sun rose, the solemn Lady Minotaur heaved up her hind-quarters and then her shoulders, and strolled off as she had come. But before she left she turned her heavy head slowly towards John, and such a grin of triumph came over her stupid old face that he dashed back into his room and slammed the door in a rage.

These things puzzled John, and more and more he came to feel that there had, perhaps always, been something queer about Greenleas. He became more and more keen though to find out what was wrong, and to know if the trouble could be stopped, and more and more determined to puzzle the whole thing out.

You may imagine this when I tell you it was a Centaur (with a man's upper body on a horse's body) which broke in upon John Lang on one very rainy evening, and that, like the rat, the Imp, the Twolf, and the Lady Minotaur, it grinned at him! It was a very trying beast, that Centaur! Its grin, which was awful enough, was the most harmless thing about it. Have you ever seen a Centaur kick? Well, this Centaur kicked as no Centaur has ever before or since been known to kick. It kicked the front door and the dining-room and drawing-room doors to pieces. The hall furniture went into splinters, and when it galloped away at moonset (all the beasts, you know, went away at moonset) it sent the dining-room sideboard crashing into the garden.

Then at the next full moon, after the visit of the Centaur, there came a Merogre! This was like a Mermaid with a fish's tail but instead of a woman's upper body had the upper body of a green Ogre. John Lang had found himself so useless, and so annoyed, with trying to cope with beasts, that on this night he had come to bed before moonrise. Indeed, he was asleep at the time, and as nothing appeared in his own room, you would think all was peace. But not a bit of it. He was awakened by a violent shaking of the whole house. He sprang up and rushed downstairs to see what had happened.

Well might the house shake! That grinning beast (imagine if you please the grin of a Merogre!) was charging at the wall of the house with all its force. Using its arms and flapping its tail. Again, and again, and again it came on, till it had smashed right through the wall near the back-door. Not content with this mischief, the huge beast lowered its head again and again and butted with all its force against the other walls from within. These, too, gave way, and amid the crashing ruins and falling chimneys you would think the horrid beast itself would have found an end. But - not a bit of it! In the mysterious time which comes at moonset away it went, and there was nothing for it but to send for the builder and to repair the damage as quickly as possible, for fear the whole house should fall down.

You might think that with all this John Lang would be a little discouraged. But if you do, you may be sure you do not know John Lang. Some people would have advised John to take a gun and to shoot the beasts. Do you think he had not thought of that? He had - and he had shot at them. But all to no purpose: the bullets seemed simply to turn soft against them and do no harm. For a time he felt most thoroughly puzzled. Puzzled - and, compared to Johnnie, very small. For at each full moon Johnnie grew - taller, and taller! and broader, and broader! But never for one moment did John Lang lose courage.

CHAPTER 13

WHAT IS GOING TO HAPPEN?

WELL, it was very wonderful how fond, in spite of all that happened, John Lang continued to be of Greenleas. On the day when he saw that Johnnie had to stoop low before he could come in at the front-door, he did cast his thoughts back to the night when he made the exchange, and he sat down and wrote to ask if any information could be got from the man from the country which would be of any help to him. But an answer came back to say that after only one week's work the man called George had gone away, taking with him every single thing from John Lang's former room - had gone away, leaving no address, and not a trace of him had ever been found.

John Lang's determination to stick where he was grew with each month that passed. He became, in fact, more and more determined to see the thing through.

He thought it was quite evident that the house, and Johnnie himself, were under a spell of some kind, and he felt more and more convinced that if he could find out the secret he could get rid of the spell. He would do it! On that he was quite determined.

The question of Johnnie seemed to be especially interesting. He had evidently existed for an enormous time; he had evidently known many previous owners of Greenleas; and John Lang began to be quite certain of another thing, and that was that Johnnie had often changed his name. Probably he had done this, John thought, to please the successive owners of Greenleas, for, apart from the spell which was on him, Johnnie was a cheerful and kindly fellow enough.

But the weeks went on, and for all his thinking he came upon nothing at all, though on the morning after the wild career of the Merogre he did feel that if he was to do anything to save the house that thing must be done quickly.

Each beast that had come had been bigger than the last. What would be the next biggest beast to the Merogre? An

Hellephant? And then? Visions of Dragons or odious prehistoric beasts coming from their squashy quarters in unknown parts of the world, with all their native mud upon them to splash about in his nice house, haunted him all the time he and Johnnie were preparing the big barn for Johnnie to live in. For if he had to stoop when he came through the doorway after the full moon when the Lady Minotaur came, think what size he was by this time! There was nothing for him now but the barn. He insisted on being comfortable. As long as he was comfortable, he did not seem to mind, being so queer.

John Lang must now live all by himself in that house, and not have even Johnnie's snores to keep him company if beasts came.

Oh, the meals that Johnnie ate now! Twenty pounds in one week would have to be spent on them very soon. It certainly was a trying situation.

But one day help came to him.

John Lang was one morning digging for worms for fishing, in the cabbage-bed in his garden, when he came upon a piece of paper which was lying tucked away by the wind under one of the cabbage-plants. John pulled it out, and instantly thrust it into his pocket without reading it, for it was curious how Johnnie hated to have things of that kind about, or to see John Lang reading anything - or, indeed, talking to anyone but himself. It was a good thing, indeed, that now he slept in the barn John Lang was a good deal freer than before. So now, as soon as Johnnie had gone to bed, John smoothed out the sheet of paper and examined it. Hulloa! What was this? It was a page of that old book which came from the secret hiding-place.

And now - on this page the blank places were all filled up with words! The influence of the cabbage-plant (which smells and tastes, as we know, so very differently from anything else) had been what was wanted to bring out the invisible ink in which the chief part of the book was written.

Oh, joy! What was he not going to find out now? Not very much on this page actually, but still, what was there was very important. It was the page of which the visible words had been, as you will remember, "Alas!" and" Beware!" and what was now visible ran as follows:

"Alas! This house is under a spell. How this came about is too long to tell. Happily such things can never happen again. I write this book to tell some owner of beloved Greenleas how he can rid it of the spell. He can get rid of all the consequences of the spell to himself by exchanging the house and everything in it for the belongings of some other man. That is how I got it myself, and that is what I hope to do; for I cannot, in my weak state, do all that must be done before the spell is removed. The way to get rid of this miserable spell altogether, and to set Greenleas free, is twofold. First: Beware of getting anything new. This is easy. The second thing is far, far more difficult. It is ... "

And that was all! Just when full, real light upon the subject was coming, what was written came to an end at the bottom of the page.

Anything more aggravating could not be imagined. It was most interesting to find that the curse, or spell, could be got rid of. That was just what John Lang had felt so sure about. And it was distinctly encouraging, at all events, to know that the first step towards it was "easy." No! Certainly nothing new for the house or garden should be got in. John Lang's courage and his obstinate determination grew strong. He resolved not to exchange the house with anybody, come what might not to run away and give it to the first person he met whom he could deceive into believing that to be owner of Greenleas was an easy job. What larks to master the spell and to have the house free! But, oh! how to do it?

His mind flew to the remaining portions of the old book. Of course the first thing to do was to place them all in among the cabbages and to wait until the influence of the plants had made the at present invisible ink clear and readable.

No sooner thought than done. Pulling on some clothes and his slippers, he crept down-stairs, and in the dim starlight, in sight of the young new moon just above the horizon, he laid the precious fragments of the book under the biggest of the plants.

He did this in some fear and trembling, as he dreaded that Johnnie would find it and make away with it.

It was not likely that during all these months he should have failed to see that Johnnie was very much a part of the spell which lay on Greenleas, else why should the dogs have hated him so? It was quite evident that Johnnie was aware of it, and that he knew something could be done which would clear that curse away. But as he was affected by it, he had to do everything he could to prevent its removal. And this fact called out one very influential part of John Lang's determination to conquer, for he was certain that, if truly himself, Johnnie was all through the charming and delightful fellow he was when he was at his best.

To make assurance doubly sure, John enclosed the precious pieces of the book which remained with great care between cabbage-leaves before he laid them down, and put a little earth upon them to keep them close. Having done his best, he could only wait and hope.

CHAPTER 14

DANGER AND STRUGGLES

IMAGINE his dismay in the early morning at hearing Johnnie's now enormous bellowing voice singing in the garden just in the part where the cabbages grew! He dared not get up too early and go out, for fear of rousing suspicions. He could only lie and tremble lest the book should be found.

Happily his terror did not last long. Johnnie's head appeared at the window and his huge hands reached up for John Lang's clothes and boots for brushing and blacking. He could no longer get in at the door to fetch them.

"Busy gardening?" asked John Lang.

"No, only getting cabbages for soup."

Had he found the book? Trembling with fear, John dressed himself and strolled as slowly as he could make himself to go round to the kitchen garden.

Oh, joy! Johnnie had not yet got as far as the plant where the book lay.

"I'll help you to get the vegetables," John said; and presently, passing By the place where the treasure lay, he contrived to tread firmly upon it and "to drive it rather deep into the soft ground and quite out of sight.

Now, the question was, Would Johnnie in his zeal for cabbage soup (and Johnnie needed such huge buckets of soup now) gather all the plants before they had had time to darken the invisible ink?

John dug up the book one night and looked to see how things were going on. Some words had appeared. That was a comfort.

On the page on which the words "He will try" had been seen some words had now become quite clear. You could read the rest of the sentence - "He will try to prevent your finding out what can be done." This confirmed suspicions, and John Lang reburied the book, hoping again for the best.

The next night he dug it up again. But there was now no improvement. John saw that by exposing the book to the air too soon after the process of darkening the ink had begun he had delayed, if not altogether stopped, the action of the cabbage-plants. However, he laid fresh cabbage-leaves between the pages, wrapped new leaves round the book and buried it once more. Again he hoped for the best.

But there was not much time now.

The moon was growing apace. At last only one more day would there be before the full moon would shine once more.

And this full moon would see, he felt sure, the coming of the last and largest of living beasts, unless a Dragon sailed in upon him; and he could scarcely think that possible, yet he feared it rather badly.

He waited as long as he dared. Johnnie had cleared away all the cabbages the bed was empty. What could be done had been done - was it enough, or was it too little? It was, he felt, almost more than he could bear. But he waited and waited, hour after hour, until Johnnie went into his barn. He thought Johnnie never would leave him alone. If he did not, what would have happened John could not think. But the moment he heard the door of the barn shut upon his giant companion, he rushed to the place where the book lay. To dig it up, to tear away the cabbage-leaves, to rush back to the house and begin to read, did not take long. Some pages were still blank, on others new words had appeared, it is true, but mostly disjointed and with meaning still dark.

Only ten minutes now remained before moonrise came, and John Lang could hardly see at all, so intense was his excitement. In his hurry he tore the page he was turning. But - oh, joy! Here was a clear sentence - quite clear, quite readable. It began with the previously visible words, "Never allow yourself," and the words which now followed were "to let go. You must cling on. Somehow or other you must manage never to lose touch with the beast." Here was a blank, but not silence. The moon had risen, and from the room below came noises, which showed that a beast had arrived! Thrusting the book into his pocket, John Lang flew downstairs with delight, threw open a door, and there, in the drawing-room, he found that what he had expected had come to pass. There in the moonshine was a large Hellephant, a Hellish elephant with five trunks. And that Hellephant was enjoying itself hugely, for it was busy tugging down the curtains, thrashing sofa covers to ribbons, and tearing the carpet into strips!

How had it got into the room? How, indeed? I cannot tell you. The beasts seemed to be able to go just where they pleased. It was their secret, and they told nobody. Enough is it to say that when John Lang opened the door there the Hellephant was, a huge one. What was to be done? John knew.

Without pause, and without waiting to think, he dashed at the beast, and unhesitatingly, in obedience to the advice in the book, hung on with both his arms and all his might" round the left hind-leg of the ponderous animal.

Then began the most tremendous fight that was ever seen. The Hellephant had the advantage of size, John of power to move quickly; the Hellephant of strength, John Lang of power to bend easily. Both had brains; both were determined to win; and during the hours between moonrise and moonset they strove together.

It was to John's advantage, perhaps, that the struggle took place in the drawing-room, as, had the Hellephant been able to run, it is probable that John would have been shaken off the leg to which he was clinging. This, however, was out of the question. But everything else an Hellephant could do to shake off a man clinging to its hind-leg that Hellephant did. First it tried to drag him off with its trunks; but John, always keeping one arm round one of the legs, shifted from hind-leg to hind-leg, according to the direction of the beast's attempts to seize him.

"What a mercy," thought John, "that I have got hold of a hind-leg, and not one of the fore-legs!"

Then the huge beast tried to rub John off with one foot; but then John got on to the outside of the leg, and clasped too high up for the awkward foot to reach.

Then the Hellephant sat down!

That was the worst moment of all, as John was taken by surprise when he was at the back of the leg. Now grab came the trunks down between the fore-legs of the Hellephant. But John was a bit sheltered under one of the fore-legs, and hugged so close that the trunks could not get round him, however much it tried. It was most exciting!

Then all at once, and with a queer heave, the huge beast suddenly stood on its head! This was awkward, as John seemed for a moment to be hanging from a sort of tree, while his legs dangled within reach of the great trunks of the Hellephant, which came feeling up after him.

John had to throw his legs up into the air and to hold them there with infinite difficulty. Had this gone on one minute longer, John felt he could not have borne it, But happily it did not go on. The Hellephant, finding itself growing giddy in this unaccustomed position, with a sudden "flump" went down once more on all four feet.

Then at once the whole performance began again, and went over again, and over and over again. But the Hellephant had no success. John was, of course, growing tired. But so was the Hellephant. John was moreover enchanted by a feeling of success; the Hellephant cast down by a growing feeling of failure. John was strained and bruised from head to foot. But stick he would - and did!

Gradually the mysterious time crept on, slowly the efforts of the Hellephant relaxed. At last the moon set peacefully, and then all at once the Hellephant stood quite still and with drooping ears and hanging head, humbled and beaten.

Now utterly exhausted, John Lang sank to the ground, and, knowing the battle was over, fell asleep there and then without an instant's delay, and slept for about two hours without moving.

CHAPTER 15

HOPE!

WHAT an awakening for him there was when John's sleep was over! All the charming room was full of fragments. It was worse even than on the day of John Lang's first arrival, when the upset in the house had been so marked.

But - the Hellephant was gone!

It must have been after a visitor like last night's that the man George "from the country" had run away, and got rid of the plague of creatures by exchange.

But our John Lang was not going to follow his example. As we know, he was determined to endure and to fight it out. And as well as he could for his strains and bruises, he dragged himself up to his bedroom, so as to be there when Johnnie put his great hand in at the window with hot water as usual.

John was glad enough to lie still on his bed, aching from head to foot as he was, and he was not now in the least surprised at the remembrance of the torn coat and cut head of George on the night of the exchange of houses. "If that happened in any case to the owner of Greenleas, it was much better to get something for your pains," thought he. And more and more he congratulated himself on having found the book, and on the fortunate events which sent the most important page of it straight into the very place where the invisible ink was darkened.

"Dear little Imp," he thought, "how useful you were! Won't I just hold on to you when you come again!"

At this moment he heard Johnnie's great voice below the window shouting to him. "Hulloa, sir! are you there? What has gone with things? I cannot reach in."

Oh, joyful day! and joyful victory! Johnnie had actually grown smaller. No more huger and huger clothes to buy! The boots of last month would once more fit him neatly. Surely this was a morning of mornings, and everything was most jolly.

That Johnnie sulked; that he burnt the porridge; that the bread was heavy; that the mutton was raw, did not matter. Nor did it matter much that in one day he ate everyone of the eating apples which were left, that he trampled on the strawberry-beds, and pulled up all the springing green-peas. He gave his master jam which was nothing but skins and seeds, and he let the milk go sour. But it did not really matter. That sort of thing would come all right. Of course, the poor fellow, being under the spell, was doing everything he could to make John Lang think it was better to let things slide. But John Lang would not! Not he! He was going to withstand everything that came, endure everything that came, come what would.

He was more open now, and he hunted about to see if he could find any more stray leaves of his precious book right under Johnnie's angry eyes. He did not, as it happened, find any more, but that he did hunt, openly, shows the change that had come about. Of course he learnt by heart every word which could be read in the book. There were not very many of them, but there were some which were very important. You remember that one of the most tantalizing words originally seen upon the pages of the book was the single one " If," standing all by itself, and lower down in the page "Mind now" was clear. Now, that page had a whole sentence upon it, as follows:

"If you let go, the spell once more gets to work, and the next biggest beast returns. Mind now that this one must be conquered, or the growing goes on and on once more. And it will be harder than ever to stop."

All these words and the other ones John learnt by heart.

Well, the month passed. The moon waned, disappeared, appeared again, and waxed once more. And John Lang prepared himself for the next beast.

It was a wet moon this time. So John shivered with chilliness as well as with excitement as he got himself ready for whatever might happen. Do you know what it is to be undressed, and ready for a bathe, and the wind is cold, and you know the water is colder, but you know you must make the dash and get it over? Well, this and worse John Lang felt, for it was like arriving at the dentist's as well, as the time for moonrise drew near and he stood on the landing in the growing dusk waiting for whatever was going to happen.

CHAPTER 16

THUD!

ON the night of this full moon, when he expected the Merogre, John had clothed himself only in the lightest of under-things, so as to be fettered as little as possible; but, finding that in his excitement while waiting for the moon to rise he was getting shivery and chilled, he dashed up to his bedroom to put on his dressing-gown, as he knew that when you are very cold you have not your fullest strength.

He was just getting his arm into the second sleeve when something went thud! against the outside of the house wall.

Oh that tiresome dressing-gown! He tripped on its cord! He floundered on its skirt! The arm which was in would not come out! The arm which was out would not get in! It seemed ages before he was downstairs, had opened the door, and got out to the scene of action. All the while thud upon thud was heard, and the house was shaking under the blows it was receiving.

Yes, it was the Merogre come back! Heavy, smooth and huge. There was no end of a task before John Lang tonight. In looking forward to the battle, he had thought of seizing the beast by the tail and holding tight on to that, imagining, poor fellow, that as the Merogre is a clumsy beast he would have rather an easy job of it.

But he had forgotten how very slippery a Merogre's tail is.

"Whatever shall I do?" thought John. But necessity is the mother of invention, and, seizing the moment when the beast lowered its huge head for its next blow upon the house wall, John took a flying leap and perched himself astride of the beast's neck, gripped on with both his knees, and, tearing the sleeve of the dressing-gown right out in the action, clasped the two small ears of the beast with his two hands.

And so he sat, hour after hour, in the pouring rain, while the infuriated Merogre dashed here and there - against the house wall, where John was nearly smashed by the falling bricks;

against the trees, where he was nearly swept off by the branches; and, finally, into the river, where he was nearly drowned.

But that was the last terror for tonight! Already John had felt the wonder of the oncoming of dawn, and soon his adversary felt it too.

The moonset arrived, and the Merogre gave up struggling. It swam to the bank, carrying John high and dry upon its head, and gently lay down with a sigh to let John roll off among the moss and ferns.

Victory again! And in the morning lo and behold Johnnie could get into the house through the doorways once more! He was getting crosser and crosser. Yes, but none of his sulks and none of his tempers could get John to buy anything new; or to repair, or have repaired, one single thing in Greenleas. Johnnie did order a new teapot, but John Lang sent it back at once with a peremptory order that nothing was to be sent that he did not order himself by word of mouth. Mercifully the kitchen pots and pans were so far undisturbed - that was a good thing; and John Lang cheerfully ate his meals off scraps of china and drank his tea out of the same crumpled tin mug in which it wail made. For the Merogre had crashed into the china cupboard where all the dinner and tea sets were kept, and had broken them to pieces.

It was a good thing that John Lang was the sort of man who can eat anything and everything, for it seemed as if Johnnie's cooking was getting worse, and, if possible, worse still. He even took to putting sugar into the gravy and salt into the milk-puddings, and what pretended to be apple-tart was full of turnips!

Well, well! The great thing was just to eat enough to keep strong, and never mind the taste. Because - what was the next beast going to be?

CHAPTER 17

SORROW

THE next beast was the Centaur. The Centaur which kicked! John Lang had been expecting this, and had opened all the doors and windows, so as to give it room to fling its horrid legs about without hitting too many things while he was getting at it so as to clutch hard.

Yes, it was that same Centaur which came. John knew it by its specially broad grin. How it grinned! It grinned to think of how it had enjoyed itself last time; of how everything it touched had fallen to shivering fragments; and especially it grinned to think of the final "crash" which was made by the sideboard when it fell into the garden.

The moon was very bright tonight, and in its rays the kicking legs of the Centaur were throwing shadows all over the place. It seemed in the soft light to have a hundred legs, or to be a hundred Centaurs all in one room.

But John Lang rushed in - rushed bump up against its side, and swung himself up on to its neck, seizing its shaggy mane. And there he sat and held on.

For a time it seemed as if on this night, too, John was going to be victorious. But he forgot how very easily the Centaur sheds its hair.

For one hour, for two hours, and for the third hour he held on. I t was difficult to get his knees firmly into the Centaur to grip it, and he was concentrating his whole attention on the firm grasp of his hands, when - oh, horror! the tufts of hair on to which he was holding came loose. Still holding on to these during one gigantic spasm of kicking, he found himself, not only shaken off the beast's neck, but hurled head over heels out into the garden, as if he, too, had been a dining-room sideboard.

Poor John Lang! This was a sad night for him. He knew Johnnie would grow again. He knew that the next biggest beast would be with him at the next full moon. And he knew - oh, how well he knew! - how very, very difficult it is to stick on to a

Merogre. Had he not done it already? And was not his poor house broken enough by the horrid beast of last month?

But Johnnie was pleased! He made lovely puddings. He gave John Lang splendid cakes. He marched about singing at the top of his voice his most cheerful songs. Johnnie was pleased, but John Lang was doleful. He tried and tried to puzzle out how he should over-come the still stronger and more determined Merogre, and the still more vigorous Centaur which he must meet and stick on to, before he could get any further with over-coming the spell which layover Greenleas.

Several things occurred to him, and what with thinking how to conquer a Centaur and thinking how to conquer a Merogre (one so hairy and one so smooth), he grew quite muddled. At last he said to himself: "Look here, John Lang, the Merogre comes first, so think about that first; and don't you get muddled. But first of all don't be frightened of him." Yes, he thought that was the first thing - not to be frightened. And so, to begin with, John Lang decided not to call the Merogre by that name at all, but at once, and quite boldly, to call him "Flip!" No one could be afraid of a thing called "Flip."

Well, the next thing to settle was how to help himself to stick on to Flip. Ah! Now he had it - "Stick!" That was the word.

It was the time of young fir-cones, and if any of you have picked up young fir-cones which have been broken off by high winds in July, you will know what "sticky" means.

So John Lang collected fir-cones and split them, and squeezed out the juice of them. Of course, he stuck to everything, and everything stuck to him, and he got in a rage, And got out of it again. At last he found out two facts - i.e., that either wetness or dry earth would get you unstuck again, if you got either of them in between your sticky skin and the other thing.

Of course, the first fact was boring, because Flip was so fond of water. So John Lang made up his mind to wear a cotton shirt with rather long sleeves, so that if Flip came out of the river he could hold on with his knees, dry Flip's ears with his elbows in the sleeves, and then grasp so close that nothing could bring his hands (all covered with fir-cone juice) loose from their hold.

It was only on the very last day of the four weeks that these horrid facts about the effect of water and of dry earth showed themselves to him, or he would have tried to think of something else. But it was too late now to do this. As usual, he must do his best, and one way or the other cling tight on to the beast when it appeared. Oh, my word! How he must cling on! He knew that the greatest danger lay in the river, and the only consolation was that if Flip stayed under water long enough to risk the drowning of his rider, he would be certain to drown himself too; and that Flip was certain to avoid.

At last came moonrise, and at first silence. Then, at last, sounds rejoiced John Lang's ear. Flip had come! Oh, what a bore though! He came rushing cheerfully and gleefully right out of the river. So cheerful and so gay was Flip that he grinned tonight right up to his ears. He was dripping wet - wet all over. But John Lang dashed at him, leapt upon him as before, and, gripping with his knees, wiped away with his shirt-sleeves at Flip's ears as he had planned. Happily Flip's first rush had been so rapid and violent that it carried him some way inland before he could stop himself and turn round to go back to the river. And all this time John Lang was working a way getting the ears dry, and clutching with his fingers close and closer, getting rid of all dampness so that the fir-cone juice' would hold. So successful was he in his efforts that before Flip got back to the river all but two of John Lang's fingers were firmly glued to the ears. If he had not achieved this, he must have been washed right off Flip's head, because the river was in strong flood, and the stream was very swift. But although the beast plunged deep and rapidly, and though the river was full of boughs and rubbish which were being carried along by the flood and threatened to force a separation between John and the great beast which strove to get rid of him, the end came, and John's triumph came. When the moon set the old Merogre climbed out of the water once more, and once more lay down with a sigh to let John Lang get off his back.

Sooner said than done! John was stuck - stuck tight!

Now what had, during the struggle, seemed to be a disadvantage became an advantage. Had all John Lang's fingers been stuck tight the situation might have been very grave, for he certainly did not want to be carried off into space when Flip disappeared for ever. But you will remember that two of his fingers had not been able to stick on to the beast's ear. Most fortunately there was dry earth beneath this hand with the free fingers, so John managed to work some of the dry earth in between the other fingers and the ear, and after some rubbing about to get that hand free, the rest was easy. And so pleased was our friend with Flip's patience in lying there waiting for his conqueror to get off, that he gave him almost an affectionate pat as the huge beast turned and trotted away never to return.

Well, next came the Centaur once more. Once John had fought the Hellephant; twice he had fought the Merogre; now it was the Centaur's turn once more.

He conquered this, too, and this was how he managed it. He chose out two nice, heavy; round stones, and he put each of them into the foot of one of his own socks. He tied each sock firmly like a bag, and fastened one of them on to each end of a piece of stout cord about two yards long. When the Centaur came he threw this so that it wound round the beast's neck (he nicknamed the Centaur "Frump" - no one can be afraid of a thing called "Frump"), and he swung himself up on to his seat on the beast's back, and here he grasped the cord and the hair at the same time. So he rode it gaily enough for about two hours. At the end of this time the Centaur seemed suddenly to give up the idea of struggling, and lay down in its own queer ungainly way as if moonset were already there. John Lang felt one flash of delight and was just going to shake himself free from the Centaur, when the words of the book rushed back to his mind - "Never allow yourself to let go." What a mercy he had learnt them by heart!

He held on, and he held on. But oh, how sleepy he was growing! Sleepier and sleepier! He could not keep awake. If he slept he blew he would let go. If he let go! Oh, if he let go!

CHAPTER 18

NEARLY ASLEEP, BUT--

IF he let go!

But he didn't. Just as he was really falling asleep, just as the last bit of hair was about to slip from between his fingers, the Centaur moved. And this is why it moved. It knew its work up to a certain point. It knew that its dodge would be to lie quite quiet, quite still, until its rider was fast asleep, and then to leap up, and in leaping to kick violently, and to send John Lang flying over its head. But this Centaur could not keep itself - quite quiet. It chuckled! It had restrained its grin, even, so as to be still. But now, thinking once more, "It is I - it is I who have overcome the man!" it chuckled in its inside. The chuckle made it shake, and the shake woke John Lang, so that when the spring and the kick came (a kick in which the Centaur's hooves thudded right up against the ceiling), John was ready. He moved as the Centaur moved; he was taut and tight and vigorous; he was even refreshed by his little doze. But how long it seemed before the moon set. He could see nothing, think of nothing but of sticking on. Presently, however, came that curious feeling as if something were happening; a sort of sigh came into the air. Was it the little wind which welcomed the sunrise? Was it the good-bye of the moon to her reign over the sky? Who knows? John had watched for it before - he had longed for it before. And now, again, at last he felt it was coming. Now at last it was come. The little sigh passed, the moon had set. And the Centaur followed the Hellephant and the Merogre into space, never to return.

It was the Centaur who had chuckled in the night. It was John Lang who chuckled now, and with good cause. And he chuckled still more and more as he succeeded in clinging on to the Lady Minotaur -that horrible solemn Lady Minotaur which had so tried him before. Johnnie grew smaller and smaller, and final victory came in sight.

But now he must expect the return of the Twolf. Now, a Twolf is not an easy or a comfortable beast to tackle. John had stuck to the Merogre; he had clung to the Centaur's neck; he had held on to the Lady Minotaur's tail (there had been an awful moment when in one of her violent sideways kicks she had nearly wrenched her tail out of his grasp; she would have succeeded if the bunch of hair at the end of it had not caught in his waistcoat buttons); but how should he hold on to the Twolf? A Twolf has such a queer sloping back and - it bites. John Lang had a vivid impression of the noise of its clashing teeth when it was finishing up the Sunday beef in his larder. He walked up and down, and up and down, wondering how to cling on to a Twolf without being devoured himself, when at last he bethought him of a contrivance they call a "pig yoke."

In some parts of the country they turn their pigs out into the fields, and if one of them, when it gets clever and old, learns how to push its way through any sort of fence (and arrives at other people's gardens where it can feed on the young and fresh green vegetables which are not intended for it), the owner of the pig makes a soft of triangle of wood which will open at the point, and putting the base of it under the pig's chin, he straps the other two sides of it tightly together above the pig's head.

This arrangement John Lang got ready for the Twolf. And it was gloriously successful. With a tempting piece of meat John got the Twolf to stretch his heads out across the proper place in the triangle which he had propped upon the ground, and then like lightning he closed the two side pieces together and strapped them tight.

Held in this way and prevented from turning his heads round, the beast could not bite John, who held on to it quite comfortably - at least, nearly comfortably. A Twolf has a habit of dancing and rushing round in circles, yelling with a sort of fiendish laugh, which almost splits one's ears when one's arms are round its neck. It was too short in the legs for John to use his own feet in this struggle. He was just dragged round and round, in and out of his flower-beds, and into the house, and out of the house! Quite an unpleasant time he had that night, when one comes to think of it. And right glad was he when the mad, and maddening, beast felt the weird influence of moonset, and sat down on its haunches with its tongues hanging out of its mouths, panting like a dog after its exertions. John got up, expecting the Twolf to go away as all the other beasts had done. But there it sat! Why didn't it go away? Oh, of course, it didn't want to have to go into space with the pig yoke on its neck!

It was rather nervous work to undo that strap. Hut John Lang did it, and was immensely relieved when the delivered beast gave itself a hurried shake, and, as if conscious it was late, dashed off into the bushes and disappeared for ever.

That was over. But - now comes the Imp!

Have you ever tried to catch an Imp?

Well, if you have, you know! And if you haven't, you can guess what a business that was.

It was all very well to say "Hold on," and to resolve to hold on! But in order to hold on to a creature you must first catch it. And the question was - how?

CHAPTER 19

THE LAST PAGE OF THE ANCIENT BOOK

JOHN LANG pondered long and deeply on the great problem, and he bethought him that perhaps the one page of his book which was still quite blank might give him ideas which would be really useful. For there must be no failure now. So much depended upon success. But how should he make the book speak out? All the cabbages were gone, and he dared not nave any new ones in the garden. The warning against getting anything new into house and grounds was too clear.

But when he came to think of it, he realized that the first bit of the book he had found had been lying face downwards on the ground below the cabbages, and he realized that if the piece of paper lying on the earth got the droppings from the cabbage-leaves, the earth all round it would get those droppings too.

So he went to the bed where the plants had been, and he gathered up some of the earth and crumbled it thickly all over the blank page of the book, and left it for several days.

When he looked at it again. there was practically no change, but he could just see dim shadows on the paper which had not been there before, which when he looked closely at them in a very bright light seemed to be two lines of what might be poetry.

This was frightfully tantalizing. No doubt in this couplet lay the most important information of the whole book.

But evidently something more was wanted. What could it be? Suddenly the idea came into his head with a flash. Of course, it was damp that was needed. The first page was found lying in the open garden and exposed fully to the damp earth. So he damped the earth, and laid some sheets of wet blotting-paper upon the top of the earth, and laid the sheet itself down upon a folded and well-damped towel. He put it away carefully, and again waited several days.

His heart beat fast with excitement as he lifted the blotting-paper and cleared off the earth.

Now for full advice as to what was to be done. Glory! There were words! Clear and plain they lay before him. And this is what the very last page of that ancient book told him - this was its final piece of wisdom:

"And for the rest
Just do your best!"

I won't try to say what John Lang thought when he saw this. I know what he did. Very slowly and very carefully he tore that sheet of paper into very small pieces, and taking the whole of what remained of the book from his pocket, he was just going to do the same thing to all that was left, when - he didn't. What was the use? The fact struck him all of a heap that he had got to catch that Imp, and in waiting for what the book would tell him he had lost a lot of time.

That book was of no more use. But there were plenty of, others. So he went to the library, and he got down one about creatures, and he read everything there was to read about Imps and their ways. At last the right idea came to him. The book said, among other things, "Next to wild horses the most inquisitive things in the world are Imps." Ah ha! Now he knew what to do. And he carefully made his arrangements.

What these were the next chapter will show.

CHAPTER 20

THE IMP COMES AGAIN

WHAT John Lang did was to sit still and wait for the Imp, armed with just one thing. And that thing was a looking-glass! One of those rather small looking-glasses in brown frames which you can hang on a nail. This he held in his hand in front of him, so that he could move round and round in every direction, keeping his back to the Imp in such a way that he could see exactly what the creature was doing. He felt sure that the Imp would want so much to see for itself what John was looking at so carefully, that it also would come to look.

So, the moon rose. And in came the Imp! It came tiptoeing in through the window, and began to look about it (grinning all the time) to see what mischief it could do. It was struck with the stillness and the silence; for John Lang kept very, very still. And the Imp began to look at John, and then to wonder what John was doing.

For a time the Imp stood in one place, peering first from one side and then from the other, trying to see what was on the other side of John.

John kept still.

Slowly, slowly the Imp began to creep nearer.

John kept quite still.

By little and little, with tiny steps, the Imp crept towards John till it was within arm's length of him.

But John did not move.

The Imp stretched out its hand and touched John's shoulder.

Still all was quiet. Nothing moved but the Imp itself.

For a few moments the creature itself was quite still also. Then it moved and John had a flash of terror that it was going to rush away. The temptation to grab at the creature was almost overwhelming. But he kept quite still.

And then, all of a sudden the Imp shot out its hand and caught hold of the side of the looking-glass.

Crash went the glass! Out went John's hands. He grasped the Imp's arm. His other hand went round its neck. And in a moment you could not tell which was John, which was the Imp, which was furniture, which was anything. Talk of the day when the wash-hand stand china was broken! Why, it was nothing to this! Before the moon set there was not one single thing in the room which was not overturned. John had been tempted a hundred times to choke the Imp. But that would not have done. The book said only, "Hold on!" So he held on, and he held on, and at last the moon set and a lovely calm came over everything. John let go. The Imp shook itself, and with a more cheerful grin than ever, it skipped out of the window, and away through the garden into the dim light of dawn.

John was almost sorry. He liked that Imp. But Greenleas was nearly free now. One more victory to be achieved! Only one more, and the spell would pass away.

CHAPTER 21

THE RAT ONCE MORE

"HEIGH-HO!" said John Lang next morning.
"I feel very tired, and what a mess!"
It was a mess! If the house had been in a bad way when John took it over, think what it was now. Think of the doings of the Hellephant. Think of the two fights with the Merogre; the two fights with the Centaur. Think of all that the other strange and excited creatures had done. The doors of Greenleas were broken, the walls cracked, the pictures banged out of their frames. There was not now a single room where the floor was not strewn with shattered furniture, and you could not go down or up the stairs except by creeping close to the wall, because the hand-rail was gone and so many of the steps were loose. John Lang now ate his food out of a soap-dish lid, and he drank out of a tin egg-cup which was saved from the wreck of the kitchen.

Owing to the shaking of the walls, the roof was beginning to crack, and as the weeks which succeeded the full moon when the Imp came were very wet and rainy, John Lang discovered every day fresh places where the rain came in.

The Lady Minotaur had left too little of his mackintosh to be any good, but he would have gone to bed under his umbrella, only that had been smashed up long ago. John did try one day to shelter himself a bit when he was sitting at tea, under the one half of one side which was sound. But the only result was that he kept his face dry while the umbrella shot all the rain it could collect down his already soaked back. And the beds were broken, and the blankets were torn - and Johnnie grumbled!

Not a nice time at all. But John Lang was too busy to bother over any of these things. He had to clear all the rooms of fragments, so that the rat would have nothing which would hide it.

He worked very hard, and with infinite labour he got it all done. At last the rooms were bare and empty, and the wind and the rain came puffing and pattering into them just as if they were real "out of doors." This took him two weeks.

Then John sat in the middle of the house and thought.

How was he to be even with that rat?

He thought, and he thought, and he thought for nearly two weeks more, and at last the happy thought came.

He got a trap.

He set the trap.

He sat down to watch the trap.

The rat came.

It sniffed and smelt at the trap.

It went into the trap.

The trap shut "click."

And John could not get it open.

So he tried with his knife.

And he tried with the poker.

And with the tongs.

And with a spoon.

And the toasting-fork.

And at last he tried with the garden roller.

That did it.

Crack went the trap, and John pounced upon the rat. It was a grey one with long whiskers, and a quaint kink in its long tail.

It had pink hands and feet, and it looked at him beseechingly out of its bright red eyes. John Lang felt quite ashamed to think of sitting there, in the middle of his wet floor, holding on all through the night to such a gentle, helpless, tiny creature.

Said he : "This seems foolish!"

Then the rat grinned!

That settled it. It might look silly to sit in the middle of a wet floor and hold on to a rat all night long. But it was not silly! And he held on steadily.

It was a mercy he did hold on, and hold on carefully, because all at once whiff!! the rat became as huge as an Hellephant. What he had been clasping close with one hand over the other became in the wink of an eye a body too big for both arms.

Just in time he got hold of a leg by slipping his arms down the back of the beast closely, and gripping hard with his elbows and finger-tips. And not too soon, either, for in a flash of time the Hellephant had shrunk again to the size of a rat ! None of the beasts had given him half the trouble these changes of size brought to him, because, so much did the rat wriggle between its changes, that you never knew at which end of the Hellephant you were going to find yourself. So that, try as John would he could never in any way be ready for what was coming. Once it was only the extreme edge of the Hellephant's ear which remained in his grasp - and think of it when this turned into only the extreme edge of the ear of the rat!

And it was a long moontime that night. Fourteen hours did that moon show above the horizon. So for fourteen hours - less the time taken to open the trap - did poor John Lang grapple with the beast.

You must imagine him sometimes with arms outspread along the beast's back, sometimes with arms pressed close to his chest to pen in the rat, which so nearly escaped with a rapid jump.

It was when this was happening for the hundredth time at least that John, looking out of the window, saw that at last the lower edge of the moon was disappearing. How slowly it seemed to go!

One - two - three - four minutes passed.

The rat seemed to know that this was the final and most critical time, and that in another sixty seconds the great curse would pass away for ever.

It gave a great struggle, and leaped with all its might. But John Lang held on - held on to the creature's very tail tip, and leapt too. He leapt, in fact, on to the stairs, where he fell over and over till he lay senseless at the bottom. But even in falling he remembered to hold on, and to hold on tight. But as he lay there, cold and stunned, at the bottom of the stairs, too dazed, too exhausted to know that his task was finished and the victory won, Johnnie came dancing out of his room shouting for joy that he was free - was free! - and the spell was gone!

John Lang soon recovered, and then what fun they had! Builders were fetched in, and people to mend all that could be mended and to replace all that was unmendable; and in an incredibly short time everything in the house and garden was put to rights.

In a fortnight Greenleas was at its best again, and John Lang and the delivered Johnnie lived happily together with three dogs, two cats, several horses, and a herd of prize cows, and knew no more trouble or anxiety.

How it all came about, how the curse arrived, and who "Willie" and "George" and the rest were, I cannot tell you. Not because I won't, but because I don't know, and what I do not, know I cannot tell.

And so at last there comes to this tale, as to so many other things,

THE END.

By the way! Do you think the tale has a good name?